Most People

For Geralyn.
—M.L.

To Beverly.
—J.E.M.

Most People

Words by Michael Leannah

Pictures by Jennifer E. Morris

TILBURY HOUSE PUBLISHERS
THOMASTON, MAINE

Most people love to smile.

Most people love to laugh.

Most people love to see other people smile and laugh too.

Most people are good people.

ONE
WAY

Most people want to help
when they see someone crying.

Most people want to help when they
see someone who is in trouble.

Most people want to make other people — even strangers — feel good.

Most people are very good people.

Some people
do bad things.
They yell bad words.

They lie and steal.
They bully and hurt and destroy.

But most people
don't do those things.

If you could line up all the people who want to be good and all the people who want to be bad, the good line would stretch from here to the tallest mountain.

All the people in the bad line could crowd together in a dark and gloomy room.

People who do bad
things can change.

There is a seed of
goodness inside them,
waiting to sprout.

Most people love the sunshine.
Most people love the Earth.

COMMUNITY GARDEN

Most people love
watching things grow.

When you see something bad happening, you may soon see someone trying to help.

The helper might be you!

Someone is always there being good, because being good is what most people do.

Most people like to run and dance and play . . .

. . . or share stories with someone they know, or snuggle with someone they love.

Most people like a kind word.

Most people like thinking
good thoughts about others.

Most people smile
when they see a baby.

Most people glow when
they hear or say "I love you."

Most people in the world know that . . .

. . . most people are very good.

Tilbury House Publishers
12 Starr Street
Thomaston, Maine 04861
800-582-1899 • www.tilburyhouse.com

Text © 2017 by Michael Leannah
Illustrations © 2017 by Jennifer E. Morris

Hardcover ISBN 978-088448-554-4
eBook ISBN 978-9-88448-556-8

First hardcover printing August 2017

15 16 17 18 19 20 XXX 10 9 8 7 6 5 4 3 2 1

Library of Congress Control Number: 2017937642

Cover designed by Alice Design Communication, Portland, Maine
Interior designed by Frame25 Productions
Printed in Korea through Four Colour Print Group, Louisville, KY

Production Date: April 2017
Plant & Location: Printed by We SP., Seoul, Korea
Batch Number: 78729-0

About the Author and Illustrator

MICHAEL LEANNAH was a teacher in elementary schools for more than 30 years and is the author of an instruction manual for teachers, *We Think with Ink*. His children's fiction has been published in *Highlights for Children*, *Ladybug*, and other magazines, and he has written two other children's books. A resident of Wisconsin, he is a father and proud grandfather.

JENNIFER E. MORRIS is the author and illustrator of the best-selling books *May I Please Have a Cookie?* and *Please Write Back!*, and the illustrator of *Lemonade Hurricane* and other award-winning children's books. She is the recipient of the Don Freeman Memorial Grant awarded by the Society of Children's Book Writers and Illustrators. Jennifer lives in rural Massachusetts with her husband and two children.

Author's Note

Young children hear adults talking, they see things on TV, and they're sometimes left thinking that the world is a place full of dangers and bad feelings. As a father, grandfather, and longtime elementary school teacher, it pains me to witness children being overly fearful of the world—of the *people* in the world. Yes, children need to be careful of strangers, but they also need to know that most people are good, kind, and helpful, and one of the great delights in life is reinforcing that knowledge through our daily interactions with others. —M.L.